# The Secrets We Create ~ Knox

## ELLE WRIGHT

Elle Wrights Books, LLC
Ypsilanti, Michigan
www.ElleWright.com

**Copy Editor/Proofreading:**
Melissa Ringsted
There For You Editing

Cover Design:
Sherelle Green

# The Secrets We Create ~ Knox

Dear Reader,

There once was a story about four men wrongfully convicted of murder. In the process of clearing their names, they found love.

If you want to be blissfully unaware and enjoy your happy ending the way it is, we understand. However, there are three sides to every story …

His. Hers. And what actually happened.

Do you think you've gotten the ugly, gritty truth figured out? We promise that you don't even know half of what actually happened.

*Let's get to work. If you can handle the job.*

Deathly Yours,
   Knox Young

*Dear Reader*

Knox's story resonated with me. My own journey to healing after my mother's death continues, but this book went a long way to help work through my own issues.

What can I say ... I LOVE me some Knox Young! And Harlow is perfect for him.

Buckle up. This is truly a ride to remember.

Love,

Elle

www.ellewright.com

# Recommended Reading

***The Secrets We Create - Knox*** is the continuation of the story stated in THE SECRETS WE HATE, and book 6 in the Once Upon a Murder series. For the best experience, please read the entire series in order!

This book features Knox Young, nephew of Victoria Young. As I revealed in SMOKE IN LOVE, Aunt Vicki married someone with her same last name. So you may be seeing more of that side of the family soon.

If you'd like to get acquainted with this family before you read, I recommend starting with that story.

————

***About those Youngs…***

IT'S NOT ME, IT'S YOU is book one in the Young In Love Series, followed by IT'S NOT LOVE, IT'S BUSINESS, then IT'S NOT THE HOOKUP, IT'S THE CHASE, IT'S NOT THEM, IT'S ONLY HER, and IT'S NOT FOREVER, IT'S FOR NOW.

The Young Family have appeared in several of my other novels/novellas.

Paityn Young found everlasting love in my novella, HER LITTLE SECRET. The twins, Blake and Bliss made their first appearance in her story.

Blake Young appeared again as Ryleigh's friend in my Once Upon a Baby novella, BEYOND EVER AFTER.

Duke Young burst onto the scene in my Pure Talent novels, THE WAY YOU TEMPT ME and THE WAY YOU HOLD ME. And he stole the show.

Dallas Young made her presence known in my Once Upon a Funeral novella, FINDING COOPER.

Then… The Young in Love Series kicked off with Blake's story, IT'S

NOT ME, IT'S YOU. Next, Dallas found her happily every after in IT'S NOT LOVE, IT's BUSINESS. And, Dexter hooked Charley in IT'S NOT THE HOOKUP, IT'S THE CHASE.

Meet their extended family in TEN CHRISTMAS SHOTS, which is a follow-up of my first historical romance set in the 1980s, MADE TO HOLD YOU.

Please Note: Several of these stories take place around the same time. Some events may happen in multiple books from a different POV.

www.ellewright.com

# Content Notes

Hi again,

I love to be surprised when I read a book. But I fully recognize that every reader is not like me. If you haven't read an Elle Wright book before, I feel like I should let you know a few things before you dive in.

*THE SECRETS WE HATE* contains sexual content, profanity, and sensitive subjects that some may find triggering.

Trigger Warnings include but are not limited to:

Violence
Death of family member(s)
Drowning
Parental Abandonment
Grief

*For Mommie, thank you for exhibiting faith in action. Miss you.*

# *Prologue*
## A DANCE WITH THE DEVIL

### MONIQUE

*A Moment in Time*

A long time ago, I thought I wanted to be Cinderella. I dreamed of Disney World and ice cream, ballgowns and "Bibbidi-Bobbidi-Boo," happiness and true love. It didn't take long for me to realize that fairy tales were weapons of mass destruction used to control women. The trick was more sinister than anyone could imagine, really. Stories told before bedtime, seeds planted to brainwash women into believing that kindness would be rewarded with glass slippers and silly songs, that the world was better with rich men, outlandish wishes, and empty calories, and that the witches would somehow get what's coming to them.

On my seventh birthday, the haze of indoctrination was

lifted when I recognized the lies embedded in the storybooks my nanny encouraged me to believe every single night.

The truth was … my nanny let my father fuck her every time my mother went to the spa. I found out because I caught him slipping his hand under her dress while everyone was singing the birthday song.

When I confronted him, he laughed. Right before he revealed that I was nothing more than a means to an end, an insurance policy that would ensure he remained in control of his father's fortune. His words stung, but I learned several valuable lessons that day.

*One.* Men were worthless pieces of shit equipped with sometimes good but mostly trash dicks.

*Two.* The so-called dark legacy of my family was my birthright and my succession plan.

*Three.* Money changed even the strongest minds.

*Four.* Witches didn't always melt under the bright light. In fact, the wicked wielded the power. Mayhem and fear controlled the weak. And I regularly enjoyed scaring the shit out of everyone.

*Five.* No one would ever make me feel that small again. I didn't give a damn who it was.

After I set my books and my nanny's clothes on fire—with her in them—my father realized something that day, too. He'd created a monster who gave less than a shit about getting dirty to achieve a goal. Even if that meant letting this nasty-ass hospital administrator think he was going to fuck me so that I could gain important information about a patient.

"Dinner tonight?" Chauncey asked, sliding his hand over my knee.

Chauncey Phillips was an old friend of my dead father, the quintessential dirty old man. And I'd used his apparent attraction for me as a means to exploit the people of Black River Falls. Today was no exception.

I crossed my legs, taking note of the way he ogled me. "What are you going to do for me?"

He handed me a file. "Can I ask what you plan to do with this information?"

Ignoring him, I scanned the notes on the first page. Metastatic laryngeal cancer. Stage 4. Prognosis grim.

"Odell is a friend of mine," he continued.

I met his waiting gaze then and shrugged. "And?"

"It's not good news for him."

"You know my father hated him, right?" I stared at him. "And now he's your friend?"

"Monique, your father's been gone for years. Odell and I have made peace."

I stood. "Good for you, but what does that have to do with me?"

Chauncey swallowed. "But his family is—"

"One of these days, you'll finally get it. I don't give a fuck about him or his family. Or you." I stuffed the file into my bag and walked to the door. But before I could open it, his hand against the wood stopped me. "You better think twice about your next move."

He retreated, shoving his hand in his pocket. "I gave you the file. What about dinner?"

"Dinner is canceled. Just like the new addition to the surgical wing."

"You can't do that," he exclaimed.

I opened the door. "I can do anything I want to do, including but not limited to having you replaced and destroying your marriage. Don't forget, I always have receipts. I'm sure your wife would finally file for divorce if she knew about that stripper you're supporting in Rosewood Heights. And the money you're embezzling from *her* charitable organization."

"Monique, you—"

I patted his cheek softly, before gripping his chin. "Old

man, you're out of your depth. I'm not my father and I won't hesitate to ruin you." I snatched his badge from the clip on his belt. "I'll take this." I breezed out of the office and strolled toward the intensive care unit.

A voice stopped me from entering the secure area. "Ma'am, you can't go in there."

Slowly, I turned to face the clerk and flashed the badge. "I won't waste time with you, Deborah Yarborough."

Her eyes widened as recognition dawned on her face. Holding her head high, she said, "You're not an employee at this hospital."

Folding my arms over my chest, I glared at her. "Bold, aren't you? We'll see if that burst of courage holds when your dear mother gets kicked out of the senior building I own."

Chauncey approached us. "What's going on here?"

I sighed, studying my thumbnail. "Handle her. Or I will." Without another word, I swiped the badge, handed it to Chauncey, and disappeared into the ICU.

It took a few minutes to find the room. Stopping at the door, I leaned in, listening to the conversation inside. The asshole was talking to his grandson. *Perfect.*

"I don't know, Papa," Lil Chaquille said. "I think Michigan is going to the Rose Bowl this year."

A low chuckle followed the hoarse, "You wish."

Fury coated my insides as the two talked about college football. The simple notion of a grandfather and his grandson talking about stupid shit grated. The Christmas music playing in the background made me angrier. I hated this time of year. *I hate him.*

Odell Young was saved by the Holy Ghost and never thought twice about spouting a scripture or anointing rooms with olive oil. Every past interaction ended with his promise to keep me in his prayers.

*He makes me sick.* I rolled my eyes when a gospel-flavored version of "O Holy Night" filled the room. Of course he would listen to a church choir album instead of the over-hyped and overplayed Motown songs from back in the day.

"Are you hungry, Papa?"

Odell grunted. "No," he whispered.

I peeked into the glass, noticed the way he winced from his spot in the bed. Back in the day, he was stocky and strong. His arms were abnormally big, almost like Popeye the Sailor Man. And his hands looked like they could crush someone's neck. Except he never displayed violent tendencies. Even when he should've. He was weak, a punk to the nth degree. A man incapable of keeping his wife out of my father's bed.

*I hate him.*

"You should get you something to eat," Odell encouraged his grandson.

Stepping into the room, I announced, "I have something you can eat." I winked at young Chaquille and let my gaze travel over his slim form. Pretty brown eyes, brown skin, lean frame. I wouldn't mind breaking him in, giving him a taste. After all, I specialized in thirst trap. Men of all ages couldn't resist. And I couldn't care less who his father and grandfather were.

Chaq stood, folding his arms over his chest. "What are you doing here?"

"Didn't your grandfather teach you manners?" I smacked Odell's foot. "You're slipping, old man."

"Back up." Chaq stepped between me and the bed. "Don't touch my grandfather."

I studied him, noted the vein bulging from his neck, the dark look in his eyes. He reminded me of his father. In looks only. But that temper? He got that from Harlow Pratt. "Pity. I guess I shouldn't be surprised. You are your stupid-ass mother's son."

"Grandson," Odell muttered, his voice raspy. "Give us a minute."

Chaq glanced his way. "No. I'm not leaving you alone."

"It's okay," I chirped. "He can stay. I won't be long." I pulled an envelope out of my bag. "It has come to my attention that you've missed several shifts."

"I've been in the hospital," Odell replied. "I followed the published protocol for reporting absences."

"Actually, you didn't," I corrected. "According to your contract, you are to notify the COO if you plan to be out of the office for longer than three days. And you are to disclose any illness that may affect your ability to perform your duties."

"This is some bullshit," Chaq muttered. "Don't you see him laying here? He can barely talk and you're in his hospital room threatening to what? Reprimand him for having cancer?"

"Chaq," Odell warned. "Quiet."

With a groan, the boy whispered a string of curses, pulled out his phone, and tapped at the screen, presumably sending a message of some sort.

I stared at him. He really was a beautiful young thing. Graceful in his movements, intelligent but slightly ghetto. A little hood. Probably got that from his momma.

*I hate her, too.* Hell, I hated everyone connected to him.

"Monique," Odell called, "I am not able to work at this moment, but I should be good to go after the new year."

I turned my attention back to the old man. "Oh, no need. You're fired."

Chaq whirled around, nostrils flaring. "Are you crazy?"

I sauntered over to him. "I *can* be."

He pointed at Odell. "This man has worked his ass off for Rivers Corporation, set to retire in June, and you're terminating him?"

Shrugging, I set the envelope on the bed. "I didn't stutter." I glanced at Odell. "At least, I brought your last paycheck. Unfortunately, though, your health care insurance expires at the end of this month. You can, however, sign up for COBRA.

It's costly, but I'm sure it doesn't cost as much as chemo-therapy."

Odell whispered, "Father God, please help her."

For some reason, *that* infuriated me. I stalked over to him. "Fuck you and your God."

"Lord, please protect her from herself," Odell continued. "Soften her heart so that she may see that the world is better without so much hate, so much evil."

"Shut up," I shouted. "Shut. Up."

"Dear God, your word says to cast our cares on you. Your word instructs us to acknowledge you in everything. I'm calling on you right now to intervene. To help me. And help her."

"If you—"

"Get the fuck out of here."

An excited chill ran up my spine when I noticed Knox standing in the doorway. It had been years since I'd seen him. Back in the day, I cut my teeth making his life hell because I knew his mother had ordered him to be nice to me no matter what. I couldn't wait to assert my authority now. "I own this hospital," I growled. "I'm being nice not kicking his ass out of here."

Slowly, Knox approached me, never taking his eyes off me. He picked up the envelope and peeked inside. Then, he ripped up the check.

I shrugged. "Your loss. It's chump change to me, but I figured your father could use the money to catch up on his mortgage."

Knox scowled. "Get out."

"Actually, you're doing me a favor. I'd love nothing more than to buy that property out from under him and leave you with nothing." I walked over to the still fuming Chaquille. "Then, I'll make your son my bar stool, right in front of that bitch Harlow."

Before I could touch Chaq, Knox gripped my wrist. "Watch it."

The warning was clear in his voice, and it caught me off guard. No, this wasn't the same Knox I'd grown up with. *This* Knox was dangerous. I didn't like that murderous look in his eyes. But I would happily break him.

"Let me go," I commanded. "You've been away for a while, so let me remind you who I am. The rules haven't changed. You don't run shit up in here. You need to remember that."

He snickered. "I think you got it twisted. I'm not my father. I'm not going to pray for you while you steal all my shit and my dignity. I don't care about your dead father, his legacy, or your last name. And I won't hesitate to throw yo' ass out of here myself. *You* need to remember that."

When he let me go with a hard shove, I struggled to remain standing. Bracing myself on the edge of the bed, I tugged at my jacket. "Mighty brave for someone with so much to lose, Knox." I walked to the door, glanced back at Chaq, then Odell, and finally Knox. "Hm … like your sister, Faith. Anyone can be at the wrong place at the wrong time."

Knox stepped toward me, a murderous glare in his eye, but Chaq pulled him back.

"Dad, stop," Chaq pleaded. "She's not worth it."

"Listen to your son, Knox. Stop. Before it's too late."

---

## KNOX

I STOOD on the edge of my father's property, staring out at Phantom Lake. The temperature near the lake was often cooler in December, but it was unusually warm tonight. I'd already danced with the devil today, but it felt like she'd made it her mission to throw me off my square.

When I thought about what could've happened in that hospital room, the rage that started in my gut and spread out to every area of my body, I knew it was time. There was only one way to prevent her interference in our lives.

Footsteps behind me alerted me to his presence before he even spoke. "What's up, Preacher?"

I eyed my homeboy, Khalil. The darkness masked his features, but the smile on his face was unmistakable. I gave him a dap. "Been a minute."

"By your choice," he said.

Once Chaq decided to attend University of Michigan, coming home became less of a priority. It had been months— maybe even a year—since I'd seen my homeboys. When I did visit the area, I stayed in the neighboring town of Rosewood Heights. I only crossed the bridge to see my father. Even then, I made sure my time there was short. Which made connecting with anyone else difficult.

Khalil knew the truth. He'd been there from the beginning, and he understood why I wanted to distance myself from Black River Falls—and the memories connected to my hometown.

After the news we'd received last week about Pops, the grim prognosis, I knew that I'd have to show up. To be there for him. To take care of him just like he'd taken care of me.

"My father is dying," I admitted.

Khalil's shoulders fell. "I'm sorry, bruh. I knew he was sick, but I didn't know he …"

I waved him off. "Shit, he already beat cancer once. I guess God is out of miracles for his faithful servant."

"I'll be sure to check in on him often."

"I'll be back and forth until …" I couldn't finish the sentence. The thought of living in this world without my father was too much for me to accept at this moment. I'd had my share of loss, but I couldn't wrap my brain around this. Someone so devoted, so faithful. He didn't smoke, didn't drink, didn't fornicate. My father rarely uttered a curse word. In fact, I only ever heard him say "shit" one time. When he broke his toe. I guess the pain was too much to hold it in.

Khalil clasped my shoulders. "Whatever you need, brotha. I got you."

"Thanks, Cap." I tilted my head upward, peered at the dark sky. The clouds obscured the stars, but the rain the forecast promised never came.

"I heard someone paid you a visit today."

I glanced at him out of the corner of my eye. "Who told you?"

"It doesn't matter."

I suspected it was Chaq, but I wouldn't press the issue. The only thing I was concerned about right now was making sure Nique couldn't terrorize my family again. "Actually, that visit is the reason why I called you here. There was a question posed at that bachelor party a while ago."

"I remember."

I turned to face him. "Now I have a question for you. When are we going to do this?"

# CHAPTER

*One*

## A BLOOD PACT

**KNOX**

*Two Months Before Monique's Disappearance*

"Where are you?"

I shot the man standing on the corner a look. When I'd arrived at Daddy Duke Diner about an hour ago, he'd been in the same spot. Judging from his outfit—new Forces, expensive watch, designer jeans—he wasn't displaced. Definitely presented like he had an address.

*Is he an employee? Lookout, perhaps?* Either way, it didn't sit right with me.

Scanning the area, I put some distance between me and ol' boy, absently adjusting the pistol on my hip. Just in case I had to use it. "What's up?" I grumbled into the phone, purposely avoiding her question. I'd known Harlow since we were kids.

We'd raised a son together—albeit in different states. I hated to lie to her. So I thought it was best to be vague.

Harlow sighed. "I've been trying to call you for an hour, Knox."

"I'm sorry."

She didn't speak for what felt like an eternity. Finally, she whispered a curse. "You know, if you're dating someone, it's—"

"I'm not. I *cannot*."

Although I'd physically let Harlow go years ago, I didn't want anyone else. Despite my best intentions, though, I'd never been able to give her what she needed. And I knew she deserved better than me.

"Knox," she whispered, "don't."

I imagined her face, the crease in her forehead when she was angry or conflicted, the way she smiled when she was nervous. Her eyes glowed when she felt accomplished or giddy. And her scent … She smelled like fresh water and happiness. *Peace.* Something I hadn't felt in a long time. After the loss of my sister and the subsequent abandonment by my mother, I had been living in a permanent state of turmoil.

"Are you okay?"

"No," she admitted softly.

"What's going on?" I prodded.

"It's Daddy-O."

The cancer had made my father's last days unbearable, but he'd refused to take any medicine, refused to do anything but pray the pain away. Chaq couldn't even convince him to try a clinical trial that could've given him more years, more time with us. Instead, Pops announced that he didn't want to prolong his life, that he was ready to "go up to yonder to be with his Lord." And I was left simultaneously respecting his wishes and resenting him for being okay with leaving us.

*I'm not ready.*

Harlow's voice pulled me out of my thoughts. "Knox? He's in so much pain. I called the hospice nurse, and he thinks he may have an infection. His doctors sent in a script for antibiotics. If he doesn't get better, I'm taking him to the hospital."

"No," I barked before I could stop myself. Closing my eyes, I let out a slow breath. "I'm sorry."

"It's okay."

"He said he didn't want extraordinary measures."

She sniffed. I hated to hear or see her cry. "It's hard to see him like this."

"I know," I agreed.

"If he has to go, let him go in peace," she said, her voice shaky. "Not in pain."

"I'll be there as soon as I can."

"Knox, we're fine. I just wanted to update you. But Mother Hawkins is here. She's staying the night. So am I. Chaq is on his way back from Myrtle Beach. I think we're good here."

I eyed the man on the corner again. He was still standing there. Still watching. "Keep me posted, please."

"I will," she assured me. "Talk to you later."

I ended the call and headed back to the restaurant.

"Nice night," the man on the corner mused.

Stopping in my tracks, I looked at him, but didn't speak.

"Make sure you try the Kool-Aid," he suggested. "My mama made it."

The remark put me at ease instantly. The guy wasn't there to cause trouble. He worked there. And he was probably stationed out front to ensure our safety. "Thanks."

Once I made it back to the private room, I took my seat, avoiding the waiting stares of Khalil, Gavin, and Sinceer.

One of the workers walked into the area. "What can I get you to drink?"

When we'd arrived earlier, he'd introduced himself as Big

Daddy. I wasn't calling that nigga that shit. "What kind of Kool-Aid do you have, man?" I asked.

Any restaurant that served Kool-Aid was top tier, in my opinion. I grew up on that shit. Red, blue, purple. 'Cause we never called out the flavor, just the color.

"Pink is weak," the guy explained. "Most people love Blue, but my favorite is Green."

"Give me that Red," I told him.

He pointed at me. "Can't go wrong with that one, playa. I'll be right back."

It took several minutes for him to bring me my drink, but once we were alone again, I said, "Back to what we were talking about before that call." The room was silent, and I glanced up to find my brothas watching me intently. "What the hell y'all looking at?"

"What's going on?" Gavin asked.

"'Cause you not gon' come in here acting like some shit didn't just happen outside," Sinceer added.

Khalil squeezed my shoulder. "We saw all those calls coming through before you walked out. Is it your Pops?"

Growing up in a small town, everyone knew everyone. And my father was one of those people who had friends everywhere. Whether it was at church, at the local diner, at the newspaper, or in law enforcement. My homeboys had known Pops since we were kids, ate at our house on many occasions, and looked in on him in my absence. As private as I was, they'd been around me enough to recognize when I was on some bullshit.

Sighing, I admitted, "He has an infection, which is causing him a lot of pain."

"Don't you think you need to get the hell out of here then?" Sinceer said.

Gavin nodded. "Exactly. We need to cut this short."

I shook my head. "Harlow's with him. Mother Hawkins. A whole house full of people."

Khalil smirked. "I know this is serious, but I have to ask. Mother Hawkins is always at the house. Every time I drop by, she's there. Is she doing more than praying for him?"

Sinceer barked out a laugh. "Man, I told you not to say that shit out loud. You know Pops is saved and filled with the Holy Ghost. He's not fucking Mother Hawkins."

"You never know." Gavin rubbed the side of his face. "Saved dicks need love, too."

I choked on my Kool-Aid. "Y'all wrong as hell for that shit." I wasn't mad at them, though, because I needed the distraction … even though the subject matter wasn't one that I wanted to discuss. Mother Hawkins had been an integral part of my life. She'd shown up for every important event, retired early to babysit Chaq, and provided unwavering support to us. I loved her and I wanted her to be happy. But I drew a hard line at discussing her potential sex life.

Khalil chuckled. "That ruler she wielded in school … She had a gleam in her eyes when she used to threaten us with it. She's probably a lil freak."

"And the way she used to beat that tambourine in church," Sinceer added. "I always thought she needed an outlet for all that pent-up frustration."

Shaking my head, I waved a dismissive hand toward him. "Shut the hell up," I muttered, even as a smile pulled at my lips. That shit was funny, and I couldn't lie … I'd thought the same thing several times when I was younger. Although, I'd never imagined her with Pops. And I didn't want to. "I'm not talking about my father and Mother Hawkins."

Khalil cleared his throat. "Alright, man. Just know we got you, Preacher."

"That's right," Sinceer agreed. "Holla if you need anything."

Nodding, I swallowed past a hard lump in my throat. "Thanks. Appreciate it." I tapped my thumb on the table. "Where were we?"

Cap flashed a grin. "I'll make sure she's at the warehouse. After that, it's on you."

My decision had been made the day Monique fired my father right before Christmas. She'd tried everything, including lying about his unpaid mortgage, to steal everything from him. And I'd vowed to make sure she could never hurt him again. "You get her there. I'll make sure the pool is full of that toxic water from Phantom Lake," I said. "Then, I'll kill that bitch the same way she killed my sister."

---

THE HOUSE WAS quiet when I let myself in a few minutes ago. I didn't want to wake anyone, so I kicked my shoes off and made my way through the living room, past the kitchen, and to my father's bedroom.

Mother Hawkins was stretched out on the chaise lounge in the corner, a Bible on her chest. I touched her shoulder gently, and her eyes popped open. She smiled. "You're here," she whispered, standing up and embracing me.

I let her hold me for a moment before I pulled away. "Why aren't you in the guest room? It can't be comfortable sleeping in here."

She shrugged. "I read a few scriptures to your father," she held up the Bible, "then I fell asleep studying my Sunday School lesson."

"How is he?"

Her expression softened. "I'm so worried. He had a rough day, but he settled down a few hours ago. The meds seem to be working. Thank God."

I nodded. "Thanks for staying with him."

"I wouldn't be anywhere else," she assured me. "Harlow and Chaq are upstairs. I plan to sleep here for the next couple of days, at least until he's feeling a little better."

"What if he doesn't feel better?" I challenged.

She blinked. "God is able, son."

I sighed heavily. "He has an incurable cancer," I argued. "He's suffering. Every day. How is that fair?"

"God never promised fair, son." She cupped my cheek, and I fought the urge to lean into her soft touch. It was the closest thing to motherly love I'd experienced in a long time. "We must not question Him. He knows best."

I didn't want to hear that shit. I didn't want to accept that *this* was best. My body burned with simmering rage. Anger. At God for letting this happen. At Mother Hawkins for acting like this wasn't as bad as it was. At my father for dying on me. At myself for not preparing for this.

All along, I was so focused on losing my sister, my mother. I'd even considered what it would feel like to lose Chaq. And Harlow. The simple thought was enough to drive me crazy. But I never imagined a world without Pops. Now, I was faced with the very real possibility that I wouldn't even have another week to spend with him, to talk to him, to hear his voice. And that pissed me the fuck off.

Turning my back on Mother Hawkins, I buried my face in my hands and counted to ten. Because if I said something, anything, it wouldn't be nice. And I would regret it. She seemed to take the hint because she folded up her blanket, smoothed her hand over my back, and exited the room without another word.

A few minutes after she left, all the strength left my body, and I sat down on the vacant chaise. Years ago, I would've dropped to my knees and prayed. Tonight, I couldn't even recite the Lord's Prayer.

"Son?"

I met my father's waiting gaze. Due to the damage to his throat, he rarely spoke. Only short, raspy words. But when he did brave the pain to get a point across, I listened.

He lifted his hand and urged me to come closer. I hesitated, because I still wasn't sure I trusted myself to stay positive, especially with inner turmoil swirling in my brain. However, my desire to hear from him—maybe for the last time—eclipsed my need to hide from this.

Gathering my courage, I approached him slowly. Last year, he was a healthy weight, still capable of picking up a block of steel, fixing an engine, and even mowing his massive lawn. At this point, he'd lost so much weight the bed seemed to swallow him up.

"How are you feeling?" I whispered.

He grunted. "Good."

I squeezed my eyes shut. Because he wasn't lying. My father had perfected the art of finding good in bad circumstances. He'd done it when Faith died. He'd done it after my mother walked out on us. And he was doing it now. I decided to ask a more specific question. "How's your pain level?"

"Hurting but not too bad."

I picked up the piece of paper on the nightstand and scanned the notes. Mother Hawkins had insisted we keep a diary of his activities. That way, all caregivers could know what was done before they got there. According to Harlow's impeccable handwriting, his last dose of pain meds was about four hours ago.

After I gave him a couple of pills, I watched him take slow sips of water before he burrowed into his pillow. "We need to talk," he mumbled.

I sat on the chair next to the hospital bed, resting my arms on the metal rails. "Okay."

"Knox, I'm proud of you."

Tears filled my eyes. "Thank you."

"I know you're struggling, but I'm going to be okay."

"You're dying."

He nodded. "I'm dying," he repeated. "But this is not the end for me."

The first tear drizzled down my cheek and I brushed it away angrily. "I guess that should make me feel better."

"That peace you're chasing … It only comes from God."

I swallowed against the sharp pain in my throat. "I'm angry," I admitted.

When I was a little boy, my father assured me I could talk to him about anything. For years, he was my best friend, the person I confided in when I was lost or sad or happy. Tragedy changed all of that, though. Instead of following Pops' lead and clinging to my faith, I closed the part of myself off that wanted to share my troubles—or my triumphs—with him. Or God.

Instead, I'd retreated into nothingness, a shell of the young man I once was. Back then, I wore my heart and my religion on my sleeves. I hadn't been that guy in so long I doubted I could even tap into the person who knew scripture like the back of my hand, the boy who prayed before every single football game and didn't care if it made me look soft. I'd seen glimpses of him, though. When I was with Harlow, when Chaq was born. But it never lasted.

"Son?" he called softly.

I cleared my throat. "Yes?"

"I know you're upset, but …"

*Upset* didn't begin to cover what I currently felt. *Upset* wasn't fueling my desire to rid the world of Nique. No, that was pure hatred. Disgust.

"You can't stay in that space," he pleaded, his eyes shining with unshed tears. "I spent so many years running from my childhood. I regret that. I don't want you to spiral into an abyss of hate and anger. It does nothing for you in the long run. It certainly won't change what's about to happen."

*It will make me feel better.* "Pops, I—"

"So tell me," he continued, "Tell me how angry you are at me."

My eyes flashed to his. "I'm not mad at you."

"You are," he insisted.

A wave of sadness cloaked me like a dark, cold shadow.

"Why aren't you fighting this?" I asked. "Why didn't you fight for me? For *our* family. You let Humphrey Rivers punk you for years."

"I had to work, son," he said.

"We could've moved. You didn't have to let him blackball you from earning an income somewhere else. But you stayed … Working on that water." The rumors of toxic dumping had plagued The Rivers Corporation for years. Everyone in town knew about that family's illegal dealings, their campaign to cover up their crimes. After Humphrey died, Nique had picked up his mantle. She didn't give a fuck who she was hurting.

"It wasn't that easy," Pops insisted.

"Why didn't you practice what you preached? To stand. To be persistent. To never give up. To not allow people to use and abuse you. They offloaded dangerous, life-threatening chemicals into that damn lake." I couldn't prove it, but I'd devoted my life to the cause. "You knew it, yet you spent hours there every day cleaning up their shit. Breathing it in, ingesting it into your body. Lung cancer wasn't enough to make you quit. Now, you have throat cancer. It's killing you. And you're just lying there. Dying. No treatment. No urge to be here for me, for your grandson. Why?"

"I'm tired," he confessed.

"It's fucked up," I muttered. "You're right, though. I *am* angry. I hate that I'm like this. Because I do love you. You're the only parent I have. I don't want you to die. And I can't be okay with this. Not knowing how they contributed to all these health issues. It wasn't simple negligence, it was intentional."

"Vengeance is mine," he whispered, repeating the well-known scripture. "I believe that God will judge them for their acts."

"Well, *I* believe that they deserve to be judged here on earth."

He reached up and cupped the back of my head, bringing me closer, resting his forehead against mine. "If you don't remember anything I've ever told you, remember this. God's will *is* right. It's as simple as that."

I closed my eyes as his words washed over me. He'd told me that so many times. I used to believe it was true. Part of me still did. But that didn't change what I was about to do.

"I love you, son," he murmured, squeezing the back of my head. "I believe you're a good person who just lost his way."

I attempted to pull away, but his grip only tightened. "I'm not, though." I had every intention on following through with the plan to kill Nique. Not just for my father, but for Faith and all the people that family had hurt in this town.

"You are," he said. "I know it in my heart."

A long time ago, a teacher had taught our class about the stages of grief. For some reason, I always got stuck at anger. Bargaining, depression … neither of those were my thing. And I certainly struggled with acceptance. Yet, staring at my father, watching him wither away, I finally understood that *he* needed to believe that I was going to be okay before he could move on.

I stood, brushed my lips over his brow. "Then rest, Pops. I'll be fine. And I'll make sure Chaq is, too."

"What about Harlow?"

Harlow wasn't just my son's mother. She was everything. The fact that my father loved her like a daughter made me smile. "Always," I promised.

Pops nodded. "She's not going to wait for you forever."

Another hard truth. "I know."

He closed his eyes. "Don't make her."

Seconds later, he drifted off to sleep. And I cried. For him. For everyone who loved him. For me. Then, I let that anger take over again, that grief, that darkness. Because now it was time to make Nique pay.

# CHAPTER
## *Two*

A BEAUTIFUL MURDER: THE JOB

**KNOX**

*Happy Death Day*

I stared down at Nique, who was sprawled out on the floor, clutching her side as blood seeped through her fingers onto the plastic tarp. "What the fuck, Cap?"

Sinceer snorted. "For real, man, what the hell? Two words—DNA evidence."

"Listen," Gavin shook his head, holding his hands in the air, "we agreed no blood at the site."

Khalil shrugged. "Shit happens. And don't worry about that damn blood. It's on the tarp."

"Was the tarp in your car?" I asked.

He waved a dismissive hand. "Look, I'll handle it."

I eyed him. "Whatever, bruh."

Nique snickered. "Y'all are pathetic," she spat. "Can't do shit right."

Ignoring her, I bent to study the wound.

She flinched. "What are you doing?" A low groan escaped her lips, but she tilted her chin up proudly. "This is ghetto," she sneered. "Your father dies, and you turn into a cold-blooded murderer? What will your son think?"

Trust me, I'd thought about that same thing countless times since I'd made the decision. I'd contemplated Chaq's reaction over and over, thought of what I'd say to him if we were caught. Every scenario was worse than the last. Disappointment. Resentment. I complained about my father leaving me, but I was essentially putting myself in a position to leave my son. Not for an illness, but for hatred.

*What would Harlow think?* We were in a good place. I was back in her bedroom. She supported me through Pops' death, helped me plan the funeral, stood by my side at the gravesite and beyond. Even though I sensed she was growing tired of me and my bullshit. Even though I knew she didn't trust me not to let her down. I didn't want to hurt her again. I wanted to stay. I wanted to be with her. Yet, how long could I lie to her before my guilt made it impossible?

That night at Daddy Duke Diner, I was so sure. That last conversation with my father hadn't changed my mind. In fact, it made me more determined. Then, Nique had shown up at his funeral, dropped a poisonous flower into the grave, taunted me about Faith *and* Pops. The peace I felt in that moment confirmed that there was no turning back.

While we'd planned this extensively, covered all the bases, best laid plans could be derailed with one mistake. One wrong move. Then, I'd have to face Harlow and Chaq, explain to both of them why I risked my entire life to destroy Nique's.

Monique's laugh pulled me from my thoughts. "Am I

supposed to be scared?" She glanced past my shoulder, presumably at Khalil, Sinceer, and Gavin. "All of you muthafuckas are dumb as hell. I'm going to kill you when I get out of here."

After everything, she really thought she was about to leave, that we were just playing a game with her. That she would just go home after this and put us back in bondage. But she was about to get a reality check.

I met her gaze. "What makes you think you're getting out of here?"

Panic flashed in her eyes.

*There it is.*

Nique wasn't one to show any emotion, and the fact that her fear had broken through her protective wall was no small feat. She sucked in a deep breath, wincing in pain.

"Ah," I smiled, "you talk a lot of shit, but that fear in your eyes is unmistakable. Almost makes me wish I could prolong this. Make you suffer the way my father did. Take away your ability to swallow without pain or walk upright or eat a full meal."

"I should've pushed your ass in that grave with your father," she growled. "You're weak. Just like him. No wonder Harlow left your sorry ass. I hate you. And I—"

Sinceer hoisted Nique up, making sure the tarp was wrapped around her. She kicked wildly in a desperate attempt to free herself, but his grip was tight. He glanced at me, then carried her over to the pool in the middle of the room and tossed her inside.

Nique hurled a string of curses as she struggled to remain upright. But the tarp made it hard for her to catch her balance. "I'll make all of you pay," she warned, attempting to disentangle herself from the plastic.

The acrylic spa pool was large enough to get the job done, but small enough to dismantle and destroy it without much trouble. It was compact, which prevented her from moving too far away from me. I stood on the top of the small staircase and peered down at her. "Sure about that?"

The more she tried to stand, the more blood she lost. That stab wound was worse that I initially thought. "Ugh," she screamed, nearly choking on the water before she spit it out. "What is this?"

"Phantom Lake," I replied with a shrug.

Her eyes widened. "Get me out of here," she ordered. "Now."

I had expected her to put up a fight. Instead, she simply hollered, screamed, threatened bodily harm. In a desperate attempt to make it to the other side of the pool, she slipped and went underwater. Seconds later, she emerged, worry lining her features.

She squeezed her eyes shut. "I can't." Her voice cracked as she repeated it over and again.

"I want you to sit in this polluted water," I said. "The same water that poisoned my father and so many residents of Black River Falls. Because of the toxins your family dumped there. Since you take so much pride in your roll in Faith's death, I want you to feel how she felt the night you lured her to the lake under the guise of peace in our families. You drowned her that night. Now, I get to watch you take your last breath the same way you watched my sister take hers. You've come full circle, Nique."

She pinned me with a glare. "Fuck your sister. Fuck your father. Fuck. You."

I grabbed the long baton I'd brought with me and pushed her under water, holding her there as she fought to breathe, to live. In the end, though, she was no match for sheer will. Eventually, her movements stopped, and her hands spread out at her sides. Her eyes stared at nothing, the light in them as dark as the water. She was gone. *And I killed her.*

The room grew eerily silent as the ramifications of my

actions flooded my brain. I committed a cardinal sin, but I still mouthed, "Lord, forgive me," before I turned to the guys.

Slowly, I approached them, meeting each of their gazes before I stopped at Sinceer. "She's all yours."

Sinceer smirked, rubbing his palms together. "Damn right. It's my turn."

———

ONCE AGAIN, I found myself standing over a bed, staring at the person in it. This time, it was Harlow. I let my gaze travel over her face, her smooth brown skin, the tiny mole above her upper lip. She was beautiful.

For the first time, though, I hesitated. Yesterday, I would've joined her without a second thought. But today … My heart clenched in my chest as doubt seeped in. Could I smile at Harlow, make love to her, knowing I'd taken someone's life?

The answer was simple, yet complicated. I'd wasted so much time, living without her, pretending that our lives were better if we were apart. I'd become a martyr, of sorts. Sacrificing my own happiness to ensure she could find hers. The only problem with that was this constant ache in my heart for her—*only* her. We lived in different states, lived separate lives. I hadn't moved on, though. Not really. Neither had she.

Just the thought of another man touching her … Hell yeah, I was jealous. *And* a little possessive. *And* totally out of bounds for it. Because I didn't own her, and I'd let her walk away without a fight. Still, I'd held on to her in a way that wasn't fair to her. I'd refused to sever the connection completely. Of course, we were co-parents. But there was always more. Emotionally and sexually.

The day my father died, the first person I wanted to see was Harlow. *My* Harlow. She'd opened her home to me that night, giving me her heart and her body willingly. Without question.

And I always wanted her.

And I couldn't walk away from her again.

The urge to touch her, to submerge myself in her warmth, took over. I climbed into bed, wrapping my arms around her and brushing my mouth over the back of her neck.

Moaning, she snuggled into me. "I didn't expect you. Thought you were staying at Daddy-O's tonight?"

After I left the warehouse, I'd stopped at my father's house to wash the stink of the water and the murder off. While the original plan was to sleep there, I couldn't stay. Too many memories. Too much pain within the walls. *Too quiet.*

"I needed to be here," I murmured, licking her shoulder before biting down on her soft skin.

"You smell like that peppermint soap Daddy-O used."

"Dr. Bronner's."

She giggled, pulling my hand up to her nose and sniffing my palm. "Yeah. And Dial soap."

I went a little overboard in the shower. But at least I didn't smell like Phantom Lake and murder. "I had to work with what he had in the house."

Turning to face me, she studied my face. For a second, I thought she recognized that I was hiding something. But when she smiled, I knew I'd successfully masked my deeds. She dragged a finger over my brow, down the side of my face. "I worry about you."

I buried my face in her neck, inhaled her sweet scent. "You don't have to."

"I do."

I brushed my nose over hers and placed a kiss to her lips. "I'm fine."

She tilted her head, pinned me with a pensive stare. "Are you?"

I shrugged. "I will be," I snapped the waistband of her pajamas, "if you take these off."

A smirk spread across her full lips. "I told you … You need to lead with that."

I tugged her shorts off, kissed my way down to her pussy, and dipped my tongue in her heat. Her legs fell open, giving me unfettered access to her, and I took full advantage. When I sucked her clit into my mouth, she cried out, immediately placing her pillow over her face. Which meant one thing—Chaq was home.

Although our son was a grown man, Harlow had always been careful not to alert him to our after-dark activity. It wasn't uncommon for her to turn up the television or the radio to drown out the sounds. Tonight, the house was silent. If Chaq was up, he definitely heard that shit. But I wouldn't burst her bubble. I needed her wet and ready, not shy and tense.

I took my time, licking, sucking, plying her with my fingers. Her muffled cries grew louder as she dug her fingernails into my scalp. And when she came, she grunted her pleasure into the silk pillowcase.

Seconds later, she opened her eyes. Frowning, she whispered, "He heard us, didn't he?"

A smile tugged at my lips. "He heard *you*."

Nibbling on her bottom lip, she said, "That's so traumatizing."

I gripped her thighs and pulled her closer. "I'm not worried about Chaq. Trust me, he's getting it in."

Harlow covered her face. "Don't say that."

"He's a man, baby."

She pouted. "He's still *my*—"

I pressed my dick against her pussy, chuckling when she gasped. "Then, try to be quiet this time." I inched inside of her and closed my eyes as a surge of sensations flooded my body. She felt so damn good, so warm, so tight. "Damn," I murmured against her mouth. "I love it here."

"Knox!" she whisper-yelled, giggling softly. "You're silly."

*More like obsessed.* I nipped her bottom lip, then kissed her. We made slow love with our mouths fused together, our bodies moving in sync. We moved to an innate beat, a rhythm created years ago. It had always been like this, even our first time. Two people meant to be this way with each other.

I didn't want to give that up.

I didn't want to walk away this time.

*But ... can I stay?*

The question hung in the air as our pace quickened. Suddenly, the need to come eclipsed my rational thought. Harlow begged me to go harder, urged me to give her what she needed.

As her orgasm washed over her, she whispered, "I'll always be yours."

Those words wrecked me, unraveled every shred of self-control I had left. I was helpless against the rush of emotions battling for dominance, and decided to give in to all of them as I came. Desire. Adoration. Respect. *Love.*

# CHAPTER
## *Three*

## A WICKED AFFAIR

**KNOX**

*Three Months Later*

Cards flew in various directions, one hitting me on my forehead and another landing on my leg.

Sinceer pounded his fist on the table and stood. "This is some bullshit. I said UNO." He poured a shot of tequila and downed it, slamming the glass down. "This muthafuckin' game. Where are the regular cards?"

I stared at him. "What the hell are you going through, Sin?"

Harlow massaged my shoulders and whispered in my ear, "I think he might be hungry."

Glancing back at her, I brushed my lips over hers. My *wife* was stunning. Beautiful in every way, from her hair to her toes. Once I realized I'd fucked everything up and needed to fight for her, I wasted no time letting her know that I was serious. Instead of selling Pops' house and going back to my life in Michigan, I proposed, sold my place, moved to Rosewood Heights, and married her. All within the span of two weeks. And my only regret was not pulling my head out of my ass sooner.

My father would've told me not to dwell on the mistakes of the past, that things happen when they're supposed to happen. I tried to focus on everything that was good about my life—not the grief that had handicapped me for so long, not my mother, and definitely not Nique. Now, my mornings were quiet. My evenings were calm. My nights were peaceful.

*My heart is full.*

She dragged her nails over my scalp, a coy smirk playing on her lips. "You better stop looking at me like that."

I kissed her again. "Say the word and we can go check on that leak in the master bathroom."

Giggling, she shoved me away playfully. "And risk a mini-sermon from Mother Hawkins? Never."

"Not to interrupt," Khalil gulped his beer, "but I keep telling y'all Mother Hawkins is a lil' freak."

Gavin barked out a laugh. "Shut up, Cap."

Sinceer was still grumbling curses about that Reverse Draw Four Gavin dropped on him a few minutes ago. "When did UNO change the rules of the game?" he grumbled.

Echo rubbed Sinceer's back. "Bae, it's just a game."

"Nah," Sin argued, "'cause muthafuckas be cheating!"

I locked eyes with Harlow. "Just waiting on you to finish the potatoes, baby."

Harlow had spent the entire day in the kitchen with her sisters, cooking everything from fried potatoes and green beans with smoked turkey meat to macaroni and cheese and chicken salad. I tried to help, but they'd booted me off the grill when I walked away to take a call and accidentally burned a slab of ribs.

The house was full, people in every open room. Chaq and his friends had commandeered the patio in the backyard, setting up around the fire pit. Mother Hawkins was currently talking to her bible study group about the joys of the Lord. Some of the older men, my father's friends, were on the front porch watching the cars drive by and talking shit. The core group, as Harlow deemed us, were in the sunroom. New Jack Swing blared from the speakers as some bobbed their heads and mimicked Teddy Riley's "Yep Yep" along with the song.

Harlow walked away, immediately barking orders at her sisters as they scrambled to set the food out.

Chaq stepped into the house, rubbing his stomach. "Ma, the food ready yet?"

She swatted him with a dish towel. "Yes, babe."

He grinned. "Bet."

Turning to me, Harlow mouthed, 'Help me.'

I took the cue, standing and announcing, "Dinner is ready."

As our guests crowded into the area, Mother Hawkins directed everyone to grab a hand. "Lord, we thank You for this gathering," she prayed. "We thank You for giving us an occasion to celebrate. My little Chaq is setting out for destinations unknown."

"You know where I'm going," Chaq murmured.

Mother Hawkins shot him a sidelong glance. "I got this." She cleared her throat. "Anyway, Father God, we want you to guide him on his journey, keep him safe from any hurt, harm, or danger. We want him home safe and sound when he's ready. And maybe, Lord Jesus, he'll come back just in time to see a new little brother or sister enter the world."

Harlow's head whipped around. "I know you lyin'."

I shook my head. "Nah, Mother Hawkins. Not happening."

The room erupted with laughter, then. Prayer forgotten. But it was all love.

Kissing Mother Hawkins' brow, I thanked her for being who she was to us. Then, I faced the group, "Bless the food and the hands that prepared it. Amen."

Someone clapped, igniting a round of applause. Harlow leaned in. "Thanks for taking over," she muttered under her breath.

I tipped her head up, stared into her eyes. "That leak, baby … We should probably take a look at that."

Harlow scanned the room, then glanced at me, then back at her parents. And finally Chaq. She quietly walked to the front of the house, looked back at me over her shoulder, then went upstairs.

*Challenge accepted.*

Without excusing myself, I followed her, catching up to her as she opened our bedroom door. Pinning her against the wall, I captured her mouth with mine, kissing her with everything in me. Frantically, I lifted her dress, ripped her underwear off, and dropped to my knees to taste her.

"Oh God," she whispered. "We're going to hell. My mother's downstairs. Oh, shit. My father, too. Damn, all Daddy-O's friends. And Chaq's." She let out a low groan, then a cute purr. "Don't stop."

I peered up at her. "You're going to have to be quiet if you don't want the house to know our business, baby." I sucked her clit into my mouth, circling it with my tongue.

"You're killing me," she breathed, perching her leg on my shoulder. "Yes!"

I reached out to the bedside table, tapped at the remote control, and turned on the television. Once I cranked up the volume, I ordered her to "come on my tongue."

And she did.

After standing, I picked her up and dropped her on the bed. I pushed her long dress over her face, freed my dick, and sunk into her. We groaned in unison as we set a frenzied pace, pushing and pulling at each other.

Harlow peeked at me over the hem of her dress. "I love you, Knox."

I smiled, brushing the fabric of her dress away from her face. Pressing my mouth to hers, I murmured. "Love you, too."

She wrapped her arms around me, holding me to her. In the back of my mind, I wondered if this was the only slice of heaven I would ever see. I told myself that it was enough. Just to love her. To be loved by her. In that moment, my only focus, my only concern was her. And when we climaxed, we did so together.

A surge of emotion welled up inside of me and I rested my forehead against hers. *I want forever with her.* In this world and beyond.

"I'll always love you, Harlow."

LATER THE FELLAS and I were seated in the office-slash-mancave that Harlow had surprised me with when I moved back to town.

The party was still raging, drinks were still flowing. But it was time for a toast. A private respite with my brothas.

"Did you see Brokeback Carlton Banks come in with his ex-wife?" Sinceer asked.

Laughter filled the room as we blazed on our old football teammate, Shawn. Months ago, that nigga tried to date *my* Harlow. Needless to say, I wasn't having that shit.

"He came to see Chaq off," I explained.

"How did Harlow feel about that?" Gavin asked, taking a sip of his drink.

I shrugged. "Shit, I don't know." What I did know was that Harlow was counting down the minutes until the house was empty so we could finish what we'd started upstairs. And the reason I knew that was because she'd whispered it in my ear when he arrived. "He's a non-factor."

Khalil chuckled. "I overheard her whispering to her sister that Big-Head Shrek was in the building, so I'd say she's unbothered."

I laughed, giving Cap a fist bump. "Sounds about right."

Sinceer held up his glass. "Well, let's get to this toast. To the devil's demise."

We clinked glasses and downed our drinks. I sat up, resting my elbows on my knees. "I feel like I need to say something." All eyes were on me in seconds. I took a deep breath and forged ahead. "My life hasn't been easy. I've been through a lot of shit, experienced so much loss. But, through it all, y'all have always been solid. You took care of Chaq, Harlow, and my father when I couldn't. Always looking out, always keeping me posted. I wouldn't have survived without that support."

The room descended into silence.

Finally, Cap shrugged, "Now that we're done with this sappy shit, let's play Spades so Sin can stop complaining about UNO."

Sinceer stood. "Y'all still gon' be cheating, but ..." He glanced at me and nodded. "Feeling's mutual, Preacher."

"We got you, man," Gavin added.

Cap clasped my shoulder. "You already know."

As we rejoined the party, I watched my homeboys, finally happy with the loves of their lives. We'd been through a lot, separately and together. Endured many trials. But one thing couldn't be denied. We were brothers, bonded by lifelong friendship, trauma, and now murder.

*How does a member of one of your favorite families become suspects of a murder? Better yet, how do they get away with it? Easy ... Together.*

———

## HARLOW

"Take this off."

Knox's whispered command spurred me into action. But damn ... *Why did I think wearing a maxi dress was the best course of action?* Especially at a barbecue. I shifted, trying to pull the fabric up and off.

He gripped my chin, ran his tongue across my lips, and kissed me. *Shit.* I moaned as he held me to him, claiming my mouth in the same way he would claim me. *As soon as I could get this dress off.*

"Harlow," he groaned, nipping my jawline.

I struggled with the belt. Earlier, he'd just tossed me on the bed and flipped the dress up. We weren't in the safe haven of our bedroom, though. We were in the sunroom, the soft music still playing on the surround sound speakers. The house empty. Our last guest had dipped about twenty minutes ago. Mother Hawkins. She'd talked our ears off about everything from tithing to potato salad. Which slapped by the way, thanks to my mother's recipe.

When she'd finally pulled out of the driveway, Knox and I let out a simultaneous sigh of relief before he led me into one of my favorite rooms in the house.

"Goodness grief," I grumbled, frustrated that my dress wasn't cooperating. Finally, I gave up, straddled his lap, and ...

"Oh, hell nah."

I jumped up as if Knox had burned me, but it was my husband's quick thinking that prevented a calamity. Luckily, my glass table would live to see another day.

Chaq covered his eyes and turned his back to us. "I exist, so I know you're not new to this newlywed thing. Go to your room."

Knox chuckled as if we didn't get caught by our son getting down and dirty. "Baby," he gripped my hips and planted me back on his lap. "It's okay."

I couldn't look at Chaq, though, so I studied my nails. After spending most of the day—and yesterday—in the kitchen, I needed a manicure.

"I thought you were going to a haunted house," Knox said.

"I came back to talk to y'all about something important."

My gaze flashed to his. "Are you okay?"

Chaq took a seat across from us. "Yeah, I'm good."

Concentrating while Knox drew lazy circles on my thigh with his finger was a futile effort, so I slipped off his lap onto the empty spot next to him. "Are you sure?" I asked, adjusting my dress.

"I'm fine," he assured me. "Ma, you don't have to worry about me."

My chin trembled as fresh tears filled my eyes. I tried—I really did—to keep them at bay. But the closer we got to this day, the more I wanted to weep. My baby boy was a man, ready to embark on the adventure of a lifetime. Without me. College was one thing, but at least I knew he was close to Knox. This time, we would be continents away from us.

Knox must've sensed my trepidation, because he squeezed my thigh. "Your mother is always going to worry about you," he explained. "No sense in telling her not to."

Chaq raised a challenging brow. "But you got her, right?"

Before Knox and I had made the commitment to actually be together, Chaq had expressed reservations about us. My son had deemed himself my protector when he was ten years old, right after some strange guy hit on me at a football game. He'd taken his role seriously, too. And he didn't care who he had to check. Even if that person was his father.

A soft smile formed on Knox's lips, and I knew he was thinking the same thing I was. *I'm proud of him.* Our son had exceeded our expectations in everything. Sports, school. He was just a good person. Better than me, for sure. Which was what I'd prayed for the day he was born.

The first tear fell unchecked, but Knox brushed it away with his thumb. "I'm sorry," I murmured, flashing a watery smile. "I'm just gonna miss you, babe."

Chaq grinned. "But that's why we have video chats, Ma. I'll call every week."

Nodding, I swallowed against the hard lump that had formed in my throat. A wave of fresh tears blurred my vision. "I know."

"Don't worry," Knox said. "I got her."

A look passed between them. Father and son, assessing each other like men. Then, Chaq nodded. "Okay."

Pulling myself together, I sat up straight. "What did you need, babe?"

"Oh," Chaq clapped his hands together, "I just wanted to thank you. For throwing this going away party. For always being there for me. I promise to be careful. I promise to make you proud."

"We're already proud of you," Knox told him. "Couldn't have asked for a better son."

Okay, so I was crying for real now. And it was ugly. I tugged several pieces of Kleenex from the box I kept on the table and wiped my eyes. But the tears kept coming.

Chaq moved closer, dropped to his knees in front of me. "Ma, you have to stop crying. This is not what's up."

I blurted out a laugh. "I know. I'm just so damn proud of you." I cupped his cheek. "Make sure you sanitize everything. Stay watchful."

"Baby, he's fine," Knox said. "We raised him right."

"Definitely," Chaq agreed. "I know how to fight." He glanced at Knox. "And I know how to pray."

Knox sucked in a deep breath. To this day, I suspected he still struggled with his faith, despite his assurances that he'd moved past it. But I knew he'd get there soon. It was in him. Daddy-O had spent many nights sending up prayers for him. For all of us.

I traced his jawline. "Our boy is grown-grown, huh?"

Knox's eyes locked on mine. "For real." He gripped the back of Chaq's head, pulling him closer and resting his forehead against his. That gesture, that show of love filled my heart with joy. "I love you, son."

The two of them embraced, and I wrapped my arms around both of them. "Aw, I love this." When they pulled back, I glanced at Chaq, then Knox. "I love you both. So much."

Standing, Chaq sighed. "Alright. Y'all can …" he motioned between us, "go to your room now."

Knox barked out a laugh.

"Um, no," I said. "Last I checked, this is not your house. I just let you live here."

Our son cracked up. "Yeah, yeah. Whatever you say." He glanced at his watch. "I'll be gone for a couple of hours. So I trust that you'll be asleep when I get back. I mean … earlier everyone knew what y'all were doing upstairs."

Know grinned.

I gaped. "What?"

"Mother Hawkins said we should just let y'all continue to think you were being slick." He shrugged. "Fortunately, my friends didn't get the joke. Until Nana announced that sex was natural."

Mortified, I covered my face. "Oh God."

Knox smoothed his hand over my back. "It is," he agreed.

I elbowed him. "Please stop."

"Anyway," Chaq said, "I'm out. Lock up."

Moments later, I heard the front door close. We sat in silence for a while. Then, Knox picked me up and sat me on his lap. "Baby, it's okay if everyone knew."

I rested my head on his chest. "I can't believe it."

"At least they didn't make it awkward."

Lifting my head up, I stared at him incredulously. "Are you serious?"

"Definitely." He tugged at my dress again. "Now ... take this off."

*Epilogue*
## A PERFECT ENDING

**HARLOW**

*One Year Later*

I loved my husband.

But I hated dust. We'd just landed, and I was on a mission to clean everything in sight. Instead of coming home to a serene environment, we arrived to clutter. Before our trip, I didn't have a chance to empty boxes, move furniture, or do any of the things I would normally do before a long vacation. And it was driving me crazy.

The first thing I did when we entered the house was light a candle and pull out the necessities—Pine Sol, Lysol, Fabuloso, microfiber clothes, and the Swiffers. Once the floors were swept and mopped, I threw a load in the laundry machine and made my way into Knox's office.

I re-organized his desk, wiped everything down, then

nearly tripped over an unmarked box. "Knox, are you ever going to empty this box?"

He walked into the office, a frown on his face. "What are you talking about?"

I finished my task, while complaining about the clutter on his desk. "How do you find anything on this desk?"

I felt him behind me and fought the urge to lean into him. Because I had so much shit to do. I flinched when he wrapped his arms around my waist, pulling me closer.

"What box?" he asked, sucking on my earlobe.

I pointed to the window, letting him know where it was. He didn't see it, but he also didn't look either. He was too busy trying to distract me with his mouth. And those talented hands.

Moaning, my eyes fluttered closed. "Knox. I'm in cleanup mode."

His assurances that the house was just fine didn't alleviate my anxiety. I promised him that I was almost done, but he unzipped my pants. *I'm in trouble.* I managed to slip from his grasp and brush past him before he could grab me again.

Looking down at the box, I kicked it. "This one?"

I picked it up, frowning when something fell out of the bottom. Grabbing the object, I studied it. Then, realization dawned on me. I held it up to the light. Sure enough, the engraving on the inside confirmed my suspicions.

"Baby, why don't you—"

"Isn't this Humphrey Rivers' ring?" I glanced at him, searching his face. I wasn't sure what I was looking for, but I braced myself for what I would see in his brown orbs. "It has their family emblem on it."

He inched closer, stared at the ring. "Hm."

Unable to take my eyes off of him, I pressed, "Why do you have this?"

"Found it somewhere, I guess."

My stomach fell and I closed my hand around the ring.

My mind drifted back to that period of time, just before Monique went missing. She'd shown up at the cemetery, but Knox had never really told me what they'd talked about. Well, he did, but I always suspected he'd left some things out. "I know Monique always kept it under lock and key in the family safe." The fact that Knox had it made me uneasy.

"How do you know where she kept it?" he tossed back.

"She told me."

"When did you start talking to Nique? Why would she divulge that information to you?"

I blew out an exasperated breath. "You still haven't answered my question, but I'll answer yours. She was braggin' on it. To anyone who would listen. You already know how she is."

"We also know that she left in a hurry."

That uneasy feeling came back with a vengeance. Everyone had heard all the rumors. The people of Black River Falls were notorious for spinning a narrative. But most of the talk had died down when the news about her ex-lover's death had dropped. We all just assumed she was on the run. But now …

*Did Knox …*

I shook my mind free from the thought, because … No. He couldn't have. I stared at him, unable to school my features. I set the ring down and squeezed his hands. "Knox, baby, is there something you need to tell me?"

When he told me no, I breathed a sigh of relief. *Thank God.*

He kissed the tip of her nose. "Actually, yeah." He wrapped his arms around me, placed a sweet kiss to my lips. "I love you."

Those words typically put me at ease, but I couldn't shake the feeling that there was more to the story. Then, I had to ask myself … *Do I care*? Would some dark truth change the fact that I'd devoted my life to this man? I'd married him. *I love him.*

I forced a smile. "You know I love you, too."

"Life is peaceful for the people of our hometown. Life is good for *us*. Chaq is thriving. We're healthy. Happy. I don't want to talk about Nique."

"Okay, but—"

"No buts." He smacked my ass. "Now, bend over."

I knew I wouldn't win this war of wills. Knox was as stubborn as he was fine. So I decided it was best to table this discussion. *If* I ever even brought it up again. Turning around, I followed his command, glancing at him over my shoulder. "You should've led with that."

As we made love, I told myself that all was well, that our life was perfect the way it was. Our relationship had endured distance and time, grief and longing. We'd come too far to turn back. Any secrets he had would die with him. And I was okay with that. In the meantime, I would fight for him. I would love him with everything in me.

*Until death do us part.*

———

## KNOX

"Knox?"

Harlow's voice pulled me from my thoughts. The whole ring debacle hit too close to home. I'd distracted her with my dick, but I couldn't help but wonder if she would broach the subject again. Turning to her, I smiled. "You're up?"

She rolled onto her side and nodded. "Couldn't sleep."

I released a breath I didn't realize I was holding. *Is this the moment I lose everything?* "What's on your mind?"

Scooting closer, she burrowed into my side and traced invisible circles on my stomach. We stayed like that for a moment before she said, "I just ..." She perched herself on her elbow, peering into my eyes. "I want you to know that I love you. No matter what. There is nothing that could ever change that."

*Is it possible to be simultaneously bound and set free*? Her words were like a warm blanket, covering my heart with a hedge of protection. My actions were mine alone, but Harlow was my saving grace. She didn't know it, but she'd eased the rough parts of my soul with her soft confession.

I placed a soft kiss to her lips. "Thank you."

"It's a promise that I made freely the day we got married. And one that I'll honor for the rest of our lives."

*Does she know*? It felt like she did, but I would never ask. I would never tell. Because I wanted her insulated from that horror. I wanted her to never think about Nique again. I *needed* her to love me the way she'd always loved me.

Harlow pressed her mouth to mine, traced my bottom lip with her tongue. "It's okay," she whispered. "I'm still *your* Harlow."

I cupped her cheeks, holding her to me as I kissed her fully. Closing my eyes, I rested my head against hers and let out a heavy sigh. "I love you so much."

She beamed at me, her brown eyes glowing under the dim light of the moon. "I know."

"And I'll love you forever."

*Once Upon a Murder Series*

*Welcome to Black River Falls. The desolate town full of unexplained events that society chooses to forget exists. When the town's powerful heiress goes missing, these former teammates become the main suspects. Love is a dangerous idea. Especially when hidden lies remain unspoken and your life hangs in the balance of destruction.*

*Connect with Elle!*

Thank you for reading Knox and Harlow's story! I love to hear from my readers. If you enjoyed *The Secrets We Create - Knox*, please consider posting a review or sending an email. They really do help. Don't forget to tell your friends!

Subscribe to my Newsletter
New Releases, Upcoming projects, and Freebies!

On Facebook,
Join my cocktail lounge for exclusive updates, drink recipes, and lots of fun!
bit.ly/EllesCocktailLounge

Visit my website: www.ellewright.com

Email me at info@ellewright.com

I fake laugh every time I think about how ironic it is to be a commitment-phobe relationship therapist who is also the daughter of two world-renowned marriage and family counselors. Seriously, it's comical!

Want to know how I messed up my life? Getting arrested for stealing a priceless artifact for a tearful client.

Want to know what my biggest problem is? Spending my life teaching women how to break relationships when all I want to do is make a relationship—with him.

Want to know what that makes me? The Break-Up Expert who is questioning everything I thought I knew.

# Excerpt: It's Not Me, It's You

YOUNG IN LOVE, BOOK ONE

"Well?" A soft smack to my ass followed the question, pulling me from a peaceful slumber.

I couldn't open my eyes, though. I couldn't even stretch like I normally did when I woke from a much-needed nap. If I did either or both of those things, I'd give myself away. Because there was a man behind me, a penis inside me. And I'd actually fallen asleep—during sex. *There's a first for everything.*

Things had seemed promising tonight. Tasty food, sensual music, stimulating conversation. Dr. Donell Pointer had hit all my superficial checkmarks for consent. *Looks.* Sincere brown eyes, pretty white teeth, strong body. *Voice.* He sounded like hot sex on a smooth, dark chocolate stick. *Personality.* The good doctor had charisma. I'd laughed at his jokes and had even enjoyed a debate on why soulmates didn't exist. Of course, he'd landed on the they-do side of the fence, while I'd stayed firmly on the no-the-hell-they-don't side. I wasn't one of those women… I didn't believe in soulmates or that love-at-first-sight bullshit. The only way to fully love someone was if you *knew* them. Fight me. But even though he was a sappy son of a bitch, it was okay. Because he'd earned a check in my most important wet-panties category. *Smile*. Oh. My. God. That thing lit up the room. And the tiny creases around his full lips made my decision easy. Sex. All night, preferably. But at least two times.

Except, I couldn't get through *one* time without a smidge of drool on the pillow, and not because he'd knocked me out with his prowess. Dr. Donnell was definitely fine as hell. Too bad he had no fuck game. No back-breaking. No tongue-talking. No toe-curling orgasm. If brown liquor was the devil, there had to be a worse name for bad, boring, small-ass dick. Hell? Disappointment? Underwhelming? No, tragic? Yep, that's it.

"Blake?" His low voice broke my reverie.

Sighing, I opened my eyes slowly. *Damn*. Such a shame to be so hot, yet so limp. A nod and a forced smile later, I rolled over on my back and tried not to look at his *little* problem. "Where is my...?" I spotted my dress on the floor near the door. Before I could slide off the bed and race toward the bathroom, his hand wrapped around my wrist.

"Baby, where do you think you're going? I'm not done with you."

*Oh, boy.* I couldn't help the hard roll of my eyes. *Lord, I promise to do better and not be a hoe if you'll just get me out of here without me having to hurt this man's feelings.* He was a friend of a friend of an associate. The last thing I needed was friend-group gossip. "I have to leave. Early meeting." I offered him another smile and a light caress on his cheek.

He pulled me closer and nuzzled his nose against my neck. "How about you stay? We can have breakfast in the morning. Together."

Shit. He just said the magic, dirty word. *Together* was not what's up. "No need. I really have to go." I slipped out of his arms. But that hand of his remained on my wrist.

"I want to see you again. Maybe you'll give me a chance to change your mind about soulmates."

*Like hell.* "Not likely," I grumbled. "So, about that." I scratched my head, scrambled to find the right words. Somehow, "fuck off" seemed too harsh. "We don't have to do this. If you haven't realized yet, I'm not one of those women who needs the obligatory 'let's get together soon' speech." Shrugging, I continued, "It's probably best if we just not even try."

"Blake, you're a beautiful woman."

*Can he just shut the hell up?*

"I had a good time with you tonight." He brushed his thumb over my nipple.

*I really have to find my panties.*

Donnell rubbed his nose over my cheek and placed a chaste kiss there. "I don't want this to end."

*Okay, I can live without my panties.*

A mix between a groan and a whimper escaped his lips as he cupped my pussy in his palm—his *small* palm.

*How the hell didn't I notice this?*

"You're so beautiful," he whispered against my ear. "I want you."

*Fuck the panties and the bra.* I gripped his hand before his finger made contact with my clit. "Okay, stop. I'm done here." I pushed him away, stood, and picked up my dress.

"Blake?"

I rolled my eyes, slipping my dress on quickly. Luckily I'd chosen the comfortable, flowy maxi dress over the sexy, short black dress I'd considered wearing. Turning to him, I met his waiting, pitiful gaze. "Dr. Pointer, thanks for tonight. But I'm not interested in more of this." I motioned toward the bed. "It was…" I stopped short of saying it was nice, because I made it a habit not to lie. "Thanks for dinner and the… conversation."

Bolting from the room, I slammed the door shut and leaned against it to catch my breath. I ran my fingers through my probably fucked-up hair and hurried out of the hotel.

*About the Author*

There was never a time when Elle Wright wasn't about to start a book, wasn't already deep in a book—or had just finished one. She grew up believing in the importance of reading, and became a lover of all things romance when her mother gave her her first romance novel. She lives in Michigan.

*Connect with Elle!*
www.ellewright.com
info@ellewright.com

facebook.com/ElleWrightAuthor
x.com/LWrightAuthor
instagram.com/lwrightauthor
amazon.com/Elle-Wright/e/B00VMEWB78
bookbub.com/profile/elle-wright

*Also by Elle Wright*

## CONTEMPORARY ROMANCE

*Edge of Scandal Series*
The Forbidden Man
His All Night
Her Kind of Man
All He Wants for Christmas

*Once Upon a Series*
Beyond Forever (Once Upon a Bridesmaid)
Beyond Ever After (Once Upon a Baby)
Finding Cooper (Once Upon a Funeral)
The Secrets We Hate (Once Upon a Murder)
The Secrets We Create - Knox (Once Upon a Murder)

*Jacksons of Ann Arbor*
It's Always Been You
Wherever You Are
Because Of You
All For You

*Wellspring Series*
Touched By You
Enticed By You
Pleasured By You

## HISTORICAL ROMANCE

Made To Hold You (The 80s)

## SUSPENSE/THRILLER

Basement Level 5: Never Scared

www.ingramcontent.com/pod-product-compliance
Lightning Source LLC
Chambersburg PA
CBHW020421150626
46554CB00014B/2329